KT-529-301

Chapter One

Harper sped up as soon as they turned the corner into their road. She couldn't help it.

"Is he there?" Ava called, scurrying after her, and Harper could hear Mum laughing.

"Yes!" Harper turned to beam at her little sister, and then gave a wave in the direction of their house. She knew it was a bit silly to wave at a cat – it wasn't as if Sammy was going to wave back – but it made her so happy to see him there in the window, draped along the back of the sofa. "I think he's asleep," she said to Ava. "Oh, no, he's waking up, I can see his golden eyes! Hey, Sammy!"

"Sammy!" Ava bounced up on tiptoe to peer over the garden fence as the tabby kitten arched his back in a huge stretch. Then he jumped his front paws over to the windowsill, so that he was

6

The Homesick Kitten

Holly Webb
Illustrated by Sophy Williams

LiTTLE TiGER

LONDON

Remembering my gorgeous Sammy

STRIPES PUBLISHING LIMITED
An imprint of the Little Tiger Group
1 Coda Studios, 189 Munster Road, London SW6 6AW

Imported into the EEA by Penguin Random House Ireland,
Morrison Chambers, 32 Nassau Street, Dublin D02 YH68

A paperback original
First published in Great Britain in 2022

Text copyright © Holly Webb, 2022
Illustrations copyright © Sophy Williams, 2022
Author photograph © Charlotte Knee Photography

ISBN: 978-1-78895-387-0

The right of Holly Webb and Sophy Williams to be identified as the
author and illustrator of this work respectively has been asserted by them
in accordance with the Copyright, Designs and Patents Act, 1988.

All rights reserved.

This book is sold subject to the condition that it shall not, by way of trade
or otherwise, be lent, resold, hired out, or otherwise circulated without
the publisher's prior consent in any form of binding or cover other than
that in which it is published and without a similar condition including this
condition being imposed upon the subsequent purchaser.

A CIP catalogue record for this book is available from the British Library.

Printed and bound in the UK.

MIX
Paper from
responsible sources
FSC® C020471

The Forest Stewardship Council® (FSC®) is a global, not-for-profit
organization dedicated to the promotion of responsible forest management
worldwide. FSC defines standards based on agreed principles for
responsible forest stewardship that are supported by environmental, social,
and economic stakeholders. To learn more, visit www.fsc.org

10 9 8 7 6 5 4 3 2 1

making a tiny bridge from the sofa. The two girls saw his mouth open wide as he mewed excitedly at them, showing little points of white teeth.

Harper didn't think she'd ever grow tired of it. Seeing Sammy waiting for them made her and Ava feel so special. Even if she'd had a difficult day at school, Sammy always cheered Harper up.

When they'd first brought Sammy home from the shelter as a tiny kitten, he'd had to scramble up the side of the sofa like he was climbing a mountain. Mum had watched him do it, and sighed and fetched a fleecy blanket to cover the fabric. The sofa was nice and almost new and she didn't want it covered in little claw marks. Now, a month later, Sammy was big enough to jump to the seat of the sofa, and then on to the back, in two huge bounces. It was his favourite place to sit, watching out of the window to see what was happening in the street. Harper reckoned he knew everything that was going on.

"Mummy! Come on!" Ava called, and as soon as Sammy saw Mum holding the front door key in her hand, he scooted along the back of the sofa and disappeared. Harper felt her mouth curling into a smile. He would be on the other side of the front door now, waiting to wind himself around their ankles, still mewing.

He was after his tea, of course, but it wasn't just that. He wanted Harper and Ava to crouch down next to him, so he could climb in and out of their laps and up their school cardigans and nudge their chins with his nose. Once Sammy had even managed to stand on Harper's head, but that was a bit painful, because he was too small to understand about not sticking his claws in.

Harper and Ava leaned against the door, giggling, as they heard Sammy mewing on the other side. "He missed us!" Ava said happily, and Harper nodded.

"I'm not sure how such a little cat makes so much noise," Mum said, as she turned the key in the door. "Mind out, Sammy!"

Harper peered round the opening

door, checking that Sammy wasn't too close behind it, but he was so clever and sensible now – he knew about doors. He'd backed up out of the way, ready to race to them as soon as they were inside. Harper kneeled on the floor of the living room next to him, and Sammy purred and purred as she stroked him.

He was so beautiful, Harper thought. She and Ava had fallen in love with him straight away when they saw the photo on the shelter website. Harper had loved the way he looked too small for his huge ears and chunky paws, and Ava thought he was a leopard, because of his dark spots. She told everyone in her Reception class that they were getting a baby leopard for a pet. One of the boys had come up to Harper in the playground and asked if it was true.

Mum had said she didn't mind which kitten they got, as long as it was friendly. They'd waited to adopt a cat until Ava was at school and a little bit more sensible, but a nervous cat would still find it hard, living with all three of them in a busy flat, even if they were on the ground floor and had a little garden.

The team at the shelter had told them that their kitten might be shy to start with, but he'd soon settle down, and Sammy had. He loved their flat and Harper was pretty sure he loved them too. He was leaning into her hand now, purring so hard she could feel him shake all over.

"Gran's coming round for tea tonight," Mum said, as she headed for the kitchen. "So if you've got homework for tomorrow, try and get it done now so you can spend some time with her."

Harper nodded, and scooped Sammy up with one hand and her

backpack with the other. "I've got a maths worksheet to do." She followed Mum into the kitchen and said slowly, "Gran came over for tea on Monday as well… Is she OK?"

Mum sat down at the kitchen table with a sigh and looked around for Ava.

"She's gone to take her uniform off," Harper said. She was starting to feel worried now. Why didn't Mum want Ava to hear what she was going to say?

"Gran's getting older, Harper, and she misses your grandad still. She gets tired easily, and doing the shopping and making meals feels like a lot of effort for her right now." Mum rubbed her eyes, looking tired. "So I've been getting the shopping for her and dropping it off after work, but it's nice

13

for her to eat with us sometimes. It means she doesn't have to cook, and she gets to see you and me and Ava. It cheers her up."

Harper eyed Mum anxiously. That all made sense, but… "There's nothing really wrong with Gran?" she asked. She could hear her voice sounding small and scared.

"No, I don't think so. We just need to look after her, OK?"

It didn't seem like a very definite answer, but Harper nodded.

When Gran arrived later on, Harper kept sneaking glances at her, trying to see if she didn't look well. But Gran seemed happy to be there, chatting to Ava and making a fuss over Sammy. She did look a little bit tired, but

14

that was all. Maybe she was having a good day, Harper thought hopefully, watching Sammy flop over next to Gran on the sofa, showing off his spotty tummy.

"Oh, are you teasing me now?" Gran murmured to him. "Are you going to jump on my hand if I try and stroke that lovely tummy, hmm? That's what my old cat Bonnie did, every time."

Harper smiled. "He did that to me this morning." Sammy didn't show any signs of wanting to pounce on Gran, though. He just collapsed across her skirt, eyes half closed, making wheezy little purring noises as she stroked his ears and tickled under his chin. "How long ago did you have Bonnie, Gran?" Harper said, trying to think. "I've seen photos, but I don't remember her."

"Oh no, you wouldn't." Gran frowned. "Let me see, Bonnie must have died when you were about two. And before you were even thought of!" she added to Ava, who was curled up at the other end of the sofa. "Then for years I couldn't bear to think of getting another cat – Bonnie was twenty, you see, she'd been with me so long. This little love might just change my mind, though. You're so lucky to have him."

Harper nodded. Gran was right – they *were* lucky. Sammy was perfect and he fitted into their home so well. She couldn't imagine any different.

Sammy closed his eyes and slumped happily, half on, half off Gran's lap. He liked Gran. She was calm and quiet, and she never decided to get up and move just when he'd got comfy…

She was rubbing under his chin with one finger now, just the way he liked it, the same way Harper did. Sammy purred hard, pointing his chin to the ceiling.

Harper was sitting next to Gran, and Ava was close by, and he could hear Mum humming to herself in the kitchen. All his family were just where they should be, and he was warm, and full, and sleepy.

Everything was good.

Chapter Two

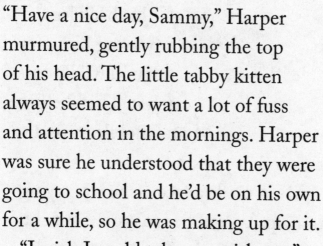

"Have a nice day, Sammy," Harper murmured, gently rubbing the top of his head. The little tabby kitten always seemed to want a lot of fuss and attention in the mornings. Harper was sure he understood that they were going to school and he'd be on his own for a while, so he was making up for it.

"I wish I could take you with me,"

she told him. "It's Monday, though, which means I've got a spelling test. You don't want to come to school today, I promise." Sammy batted at the end of her ponytail and Harper twirled it round for him, laughing as he sat up on his back legs, waving his paws around wildly to catch it. Then he froze as Mum's mobile started to ring in her pocket.

Mum made a face – she was trying to help Ava get her coat on – but she answered the phone with one hand

and held Ava's sleeve out for her with the other. "Hello? Yes… Oh! Oh no…"

Harper looked round at her, and so did Ava, caught by the panic in Mum's voice.

"Yes. I'll be there as soon as I can."

"What is it?" Harper asked, and Ava stared at Mum, her eyes round with worry.

"That was the hospital. Gran's had a fall." Mum zipped Ava's coat up tight and grabbed her backpack. "It's OK. It's OK. But I need to drop you two at school and head over there as quick as I can. I'll have to cancel my shift at the shop, but they'll understand…"

"Can't we come with you?" Harper asked, her voice very small. She was thinking of how tired and slow Gran had seemed over the last few weeks. How Mum had needed to help her up off the sofa when she came for tea a few days before.

Mum patted her cheek. "I know you're worried, love, but I don't think it's a good idea for you two to come to the hospital. We don't know what's happening and you'd probably just have to sit in a waiting room. They're looking after her, Harper, she's in the best place."

Harper knew Mum was right – but it didn't make her feel much better.

They dashed out of the house, and for once, Harper was too distracted to blow kisses to Sammy, sitting on the back of the sofa, watching them go.

Mum had phoned Harper and Ava's school later that morning to let them know that Gran was all right – she'd broken her wrist, and she had bumps and bruises, but there was nothing more serious going on. Harper was still worried, though, and she dashed out of school at the end of the day, hoping that Mum would have more news.

"How's Gran?" she asked, as soon as she spotted Mum in the playground.

Mum smiled at her and waved at Ava, who was looking round for them. "Over here, Ava! She's doing well – actually, I've got the car so we can go and see her."

"At the hospital?" Ava sounded scared.

"Yes, but it's OK, Ava. Gran's not feeling too bad and they're hoping she can come home in a few days."

"We can cheer her up," Harper said, putting her arm round her little sister. "I bet it's boring in hospital."

"Exactly." Mum nodded. "But we have to be gentle, Ava, remember. No bouncing around and disturbing people."

Ava was mouse-quiet for the whole car ride and the long walk through the hospital corridors. Harper had been there once before when she fell off her friend Maya's trampoline, but that was only to A&E – the rest of the hospital was enormous and Gran's ward seemed to be miles from the car park. It was very quiet, and Harper felt like they ought to be walking on tiptoe as Mum led them over to Gran's bed.

"You brought them!" Gran was beaming and Harper immediately felt better. She'd been expecting Gran to look really ill, but she seemed fine apart from the cast on her wrist and she was so pleased to see them.

Mum let Ava chatter to Gran for a couple of minutes about the forest school lesson her class had done, and then she broke in – Ava's stories could go on for a while. "Listen, girls. We need to talk to you. Gran and I have been thinking…"

Harper looked at her worriedly – there was something in Mum's voice, something that meant this was serious.

Gran smiled at her. "We've had an idea. Don't panic, Harper. Let your mum explain."

"Gran's got lots of space at her house and she's feeling a bit lonely, now it's harder work for her to go out. And it would be good if there was someone else around, just in case she has another fall. So … we were thinking that perhaps we

26

should move in. With Gran."

"But what about our flat?" Harper said, frowning. They'd lived in the flat for so long – she could hardly remember the house they'd had before, when they still lived with their dad as well as their mum.

"Well, it wouldn't be our flat any more. Someone else would rent it and we'd live in Gran's house."

"You could have your own bedrooms. You wouldn't have to share," Gran put in, smiling at Harper and Ava.

"My own room!" Ava squeaked. "Can I have purple paint?"

"Maybe." Mum laughed. "Harper? What do you think? I know it's a big change, but you'd love your own room, wouldn't you? And Gran's house is closer to school. Less of a rush in the mornings."

Harper stared at the blanket on the hospital bed and tried to imagine living in Gran's house, with all their things…

"What about Sammy?" she burst out.

Gran reached out and laid her good hand over Harper's. "That would be another lovely thing for me," she said. "I'd have you two and your mum, and I'd have a cat around again. I'm sure he'll be fine, Harper. He's only been with you, what, five weeks? He's young enough to get used to somewhere new."

"We'd keep him indoors at Gran's for a few days," Mum added. "Just till he's settled."

Harper nodded, a little doubtfully. Sammy loved their tiny garden. He spent ages sunbathing and trying to catch bees. He wasn't going to be very happy about staying inside. She realized Mum was right, though. He was going to be really confused when he went out through Bonnie's old catflap and found himself in a whole new garden. It would be better if he got used to Gran's house first.

"When are we going to move?" Harper asked. She still wasn't sure how she felt about the idea. Even though it made sense, and she definitely wanted to help Mum look after Gran, it was such a big change. She needed time to think about it.

Mum and Gran exchanged a look. "Soon," Mum said gently.

"The doctor we spoke to thinks I need someone to look after me when I come home from the hospital," Gran explained.

"But … you said that would just be in a few days!" Harper's voice was a surprised squeak.

Mum nodded. "I'm going to speak to the owner of our flat and explain. We're going to try and move this week."

This week! Harper tried to nod, and smile, but she couldn't imagine living somewhere different in just a few days' time.

Sammy watched uncertainly as yet another bag was piled up in the little hallway of the flat. He wasn't sure what was going on. He liked the bags and boxes – he could jump up and sit on top of them, and then he was higher than everyone else, and that was very good. He was sure there was more to the boxes than that, though.

Every time he padded into a room, it seemed to have changed. Furniture kept moving around and the flat even smelled different, he was sure. This morning, Mum had whipped his food bowl away as soon as he'd finished eating – she hadn't even given him time to wash his whiskers. The blanket that he liked to lie on along the back of the sofa had disappeared too and there were no baskets of washing around to sleep in. Everywhere he looked something was wrong and he hated it.

He marched crossly over to Harper, ears flattened and tail whipping, and rubbed the side of his head against her socks. She crouched down to stroke his ears, just the way he liked, but she wasn't looking at him, she was still talking to Mum. He didn't like the way her voice sounded – shaky and worried.

"It's going to be so weird. Coming home to Gran's house after school."

"It's strange for me as well, Harper. I know it's a huge change." Mum sounded different too and Sammy edged away a little.

"I'm getting my new room today!"
Ava screeched, jumping from the
bottom step of the stairs and throwing
her arms round Mum's waist.

Sammy darted back, his tail fluffing
up wildly. Harper and Mum were
laughing, but there was an odd feeling
in the air, he was sure of it. Everything
felt jangly and sharp, and it was
frightening him.

He slipped in between two of the

huge boxes, squeezing into the narrow space. It was better, there in the dark. He watched Harper and Ava and Mum set out for school, and he hoped and hoped that everything would be right again when they came back.

Chapter Three

Sammy had been in his cat basket a
few times – that first terrifying journey
back from the shelter, which he hardly
remembered, and then to the vet for
his jabs. He hated it every time. He
was bigger now than when he'd first
travelled in the basket, and braver, so
he'd wriggled and squirmed and almost
managed to duck under Mum's hands,

but she'd got the wire door closed just before he managed to dart out of it.

Sammy yowled furiously for most of the drive. He was expecting to be at the vet's again when they got out of the car, but it was somewhere entirely new. He stalked out of the basket, stiff-legged and angry. There was a tiled kitchen floor and piles of boxes everywhere, again!

"Hey, Sammy... It's OK. Don't worry..."

Sammy glanced up at Mum. Where were they, and why was Mum here, but not Harper or Ava? What was going on? He was so cross that the fur lifted up all along his spine.

"I'm sure you'll get used to it soon," Mum said gently, and she stroked him, smoothing down the fluffed-up fur and making him feel a little better. He rubbed his chin against her hand and closed his eyes against the strangeness for a moment. She was familiar, at least. Mum fussed around with boxes while Sammy sniffed cautiously at things in the kitchen.

"Here you are, kitten," Mum said, putting his water bowl down next to him. Sammy stared at it. That was his bowl, the bowl he drank from every day at home. What was it doing here?

"Let's give you a little bit of the special food as well," Mum murmured. "That expensive stuff in the tins that Harper and Ava wanted to get for you. I found it when I was clearing out the kitchen cupboards..." She rummaged

in a box on the table for a moment
and then put Sammy's food bowl
down in front of him, with something
that smelled strong and delicious. But
Sammy backed away from her. He was
hungry, but he didn't want to eat here.
This felt all wrong…

"Oh, Sammy." Mum looked at him
worriedly. "Harper and Ava will be
back soon, perhaps that'll cheer you
up."

Sammy retreated under the kitchen table, where he thought no one could reach him. He sat there all hunched up, glaring at Mum's feet as she hurried around, opening boxes. More things that seemed familiar appeared – there were smells he recognized, smells of home. Why were all these home things here, when this was not home?

When Mum left the kitchen, pulling on the coat she'd left over the back of a chair, Sammy edged out after her, wondering if she was going home. Wasn't she going to take him too? He mewed worriedly at her and Mum darted over to give him one last quick pat.

"Back soon, Sammy. I'm going to pick up Gran from the hospital and then get the girls from school. I've got to go, I'll be late!"

She hurried out, banging the door hard behind her, and Sammy was left alone, staring around him in bewilderment.

At last he padded back down the hallway, peeping into rooms and sneezing at the dusty furniture. The house felt big, and empty, and wrong...

Harper wasn't sure what to feel when she and Ava got out of school. She was excited and worried and sad all at once.

Her own room! She didn't mind sharing with Ava that much – it was cute sometimes when her little sister wanted to climb into bed with her in the mornings. But she always had to put her precious things up on a high shelf, just so Ava wouldn't mess around with them. It wasn't that her sister meant to break things, she couldn't help it, being little and a bit careless. But now there would be no more Ava deciding to borrow her best pens, just because they were there, and leaving the lids off. No more scribbled-on homework.

It was going to be nice getting to live with Gran too, especially now she needed extra help. They wouldn't have to worry about Gran being lonely, or maybe having another fall with no one there to look after her. Gran was beaming at them from the front seat of the car – she looked so happy that they were all going to be together.

The flat, though… It was home.
Harper wished the rental agency hadn't
wanted them to move out on a school
day. Even though they'd been able to
take things over to Gran's ever since
they'd decided on leaving, a few days
before, it had still been a rush that
morning, trying to wash and have
breakfast in a flat that was almost all
packed up. She didn't feel like she'd
had time to say goodbye properly.

At least she'd known what was going on, though. Poor Sammy must have been so confused. She nibbled her bottom lip, listening to Mum explain to Ava that yes, the movers had put her bed in her new room, and her dolls' house, and her pirate outfit...

"Is Sammy OK?" Harper broke in, when Ava stopped asking questions to breathe. "Does he like it at Gran's?"

Mum sighed. "Ummm, I think he's a bit cross. He didn't want anything to eat earlier on – but we have to give him some time to get used to a new home, Harper. Don't worry. I'm sure he'll be fine."

Harper nodded, but she was still chewing her bottom lip. Mum loved Sammy, Harper knew that she did, but it wasn't the same. Harper was the one who played with him most, and always came down in the morning to feed him. She groomed him and even cleaned out his litter tray. Sammy slept on her bed most nights now. She couldn't help feeling that Sammy was mostly hers. She had to make sure he was OK.

When they pulled up outside the house, Ava bounced out of the car and twirled her way to the doorstep, obviously desperate to run and see her new room now it had her things in.

Mum unlocked the door and helped Gran inside, and they hung up their jackets on the hooks – they'd done that so many times before, but this time it was different. This was their home too, now.

Harper had hoped Sammy would come bounding towards her, like he usually did, but no little grey spotted cat raced down the hallway.

"He's behind the basket, there," Gran murmured behind her, and then when Harper looked up at her in surprise, she smiled. "I could see you looking around for him. Don't worry, Harper. He'll get used to the new place soon."

Harper nodded, smiling back, and then she crouched down to peer round the basket. A small, cross, stripey face glared back at her. Harper really wanted to reach in and pick Sammy up, but she thought she'd better leave him to come out in his own time. He was grumpy already. He didn't want to be grabbed.

"I could get you your tea," she whispered to him, her voice soft and persuasive. "Would you like that?"

Mum looked round – she was halfway up the stairs, following Ava. "I put some food down for him before, Harper, one of those posh little tins. Maybe change it for something else? Perhaps he just wants his normal biscuits? I'll be down in a minute, Mum. I'll make you a cup of tea."

Harper nodded. And then realized she didn't even know where the bag of

46

cat food was, in Gran's kitchen, and sighed. No wonder Sammy was upset.

"Come on, love." Gran took her hand. "Let your mum sort Ava out. She's got enough to worry about, I can manage putting the kettle on, and I'm sure there's juice in the fridge. I could pour you some while you see where she's put the cat food. And you can tell me what your day was like. I'd love that."

Harper stood up, glancing back at the basket. Maybe she was getting worked up over nothing. Gran knew about cats and she thought Sammy would be fine.

"He'll be here any minute," Gran reassured her, as Harper opened cupboard doors, searching for the cat food. It was in the cupboard by the sink, just like it had been at home – Harper frowned at herself – at the old flat, she meant. She had to start thinking of this house as home now. They all did.

She pulled the bag out, hearing it rustle, and looked hopefully towards the hall. Yes… There he was by the basket – peeping round to check what was going on. Harper rustled the bag a bit more, on purpose, and then gave Gran a big grin of relief as Sammy came trotting purposefully down the hall.

Maybe everything *was* going to be all right?

Chapter Four

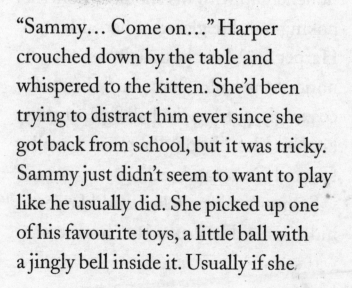

"Sammy… Come on…" Harper crouched down by the table and whispered to the kitten. She'd been trying to distract him ever since she got back from school, but it was tricky. Sammy just didn't seem to want to play like he usually did. She picked up one of his favourite toys, a little ball with a jingly bell inside it. Usually if she rolled it for him he'd race after it and leap on it, as if it was some sort of fierce monster he had to squish. Sometimes he even tried picking it up in his paws and ended up doing kitten juggling. He always made Harper laugh.

"Look, Sammy... I've got your ball," she said, holding it up hopefully. Sammy was sitting by the cat flap, hunched up with his shoulder bones all poking out. He glared at her, although Harper could see he'd definitely noticed the ball. "Come on," she said coaxingly, patting the ball against the kitchen tiles. "Look! I'm going to roll it for you! Come and see!"

Sammy's tail twitched and Harper hid a smile. He *wanted* to chase it, she was sure.

She'd really hoped that after a week Sammy would be settling into their new home, but it just didn't seem to be happening. He kept tracking round the house, as though he was searching for something, and he was totally confused by the stairs. He spent ages sitting next to the bottom step and staring up, and he hadn't tried climbing them yet. Harper wanted so much to pick him up and take him to see her new

51

bedroom, but she'd resisted. Sammy would get up there eventually, she told herself. It was just that she missed him curling up to sleep in the space behind her knees.

Sammy really didn't like being shut indoors, either. He spent a lot of time sitting by the locked cat flap in the kitchen and banging it with his paw. Then he would look round at Harper accusingly. She usually managed to distract him with a toy or a treat, but she was pretty sure that while she was at school he'd spent a lot of his time scratching the cat flap and trying to get into the garden. Gran was still feeling tired and a bit wobbly after her fall, and she couldn't keep getting up to come and fuss over him.

Harper could understand that
Sammy didn't like being shut up. She
wouldn't want to be indoors all the
time, either, but they had to wait until
he was settled in. Mum had looked it
up and said she thought a week was
long enough, so he'd be able to go out
in the garden at the weekend, when
someone could be with him to make
sure he didn't dash off and get lost.

At least now it was Friday afternoon
and Harper could spend some more
time with him over the weekend.

"Harper, have you finished your
unpacking yet?" Mum walked into
the kitchen, pushing her hair off her
forehead with one hand. She'd been
busy all week trying to get everyone
settled, and keeping an eye on Gran,

and going to work. Now she looked hot and harassed. Harper glanced up guiltily. She hadn't put away much of her stuff at all — just a few clothes — the boxes were still piled up in her room.

"I was trying to cheer Sammy up…"

"I know, love, but those boxes have to go back to the movers, remember? Can you go and start doing it, please?"

"Can't I do it tomorrow?" Harper

pleaded. "I'll have loads of time then. I nearly got Sammy to play with his ball a minute ago."

"Except tomorrow you wanted to let him out in the garden," Mum reminded her. "You'll need to be out there keeping an eye on him, won't you? He'll be fine for now, Harper, and it'll definitely cheer him up going outside in the morning."

Harper sighed and headed upstairs. She knew Mum had been unpacking and tidying and working all day, but she'd been at school, which was work too. No one seemed to be worried about Sammy like she was. It just wasn't fair.

Sammy padded into the living room, his tail twitching miserably. He'd been about to chase his ball, but then Harper had gone again, up the stairs. He didn't like stairs, they felt different, and wrong… His home didn't have stairs.

Gran was there, sitting in her favourite chair with a magazine, and she stretched out her hand to him. Sammy bumped his head against her fingers, but he didn't leap up on to her lap. He still felt edgy, and confused, and cross – and even worse, he needed to wee. Back at the flat, he'd have used his litter tray, or popped out of the cat flap to the garden, but here it was more difficult. The cat flap didn't work, however much he'd scrabbled at it, and his litter tray kept moving around.

It had been in a corner of the kitchen, and then in a little room next door, and now he wasn't sure where it had disappeared to.

He really needed to go. He clawed at the rug, over in the corner of the room away from Gran. It wasn't the right thing to do, he knew that – but he couldn't help it! What was he supposed to do, if they wouldn't let him out? He glanced around guiltily and heard a worried gasp from Gran as he started to wee.

"Oh dear, don't do that, Sammy…"

It was too late. Sammy scratched at the rug again and then scooted behind the sofa, feeling upset.

"Emma!" Gran struggled up from her chair, and went out into the hallway, leaving Sammy lurking behind the sofa. He could smell the wet patch he'd left on the rug and it smelled wrong, not like his litter tray. He shouldn't have done it.

"What's up? Are you OK?" Mum called down from the landing, and then Sammy heard her hurrying downstairs.

"Yes, yes, I'm fine, don't panic, love. But Sammy's had an accident."

"An accident?" Sammy heard Harper's voice, sounding sharp and worried. "Is he hurt?"

"Not that sort of an accident. He's fine, but he did a wee on the living-room rug."

"Oh no…" Mum sighed. "That's just what we need." She came into the living room and crouched down by the rug. Sammy watched her miserably. He could tell that she was upset. "Will this go in the washing machine? I'm so sorry, Mum. Honestly, why on earth would he do that?"

"It isn't his fault!" Harper marched across the room to stand next to Mum, and Sammy flinched at her cross voice. Had he made her sound like that? "I told you he wasn't happy!"

"That doesn't mean he ought to go and wee all over the place!" Mum snapped back. "And don't use that rude tone, please."

"But I did tell you!"

"Harper!"

Ava appeared in the doorway and peered in. "Mummy, why are you shouting? What did Harper do?"

"Mind your own business!" Harper growled.

"I think it's my fault," Gran put in, and Sammy felt his prickly fur settle a bit. Mum and Harper seemed to be caught by her soft voice too, and they spun round to look at her. "I emptied his litter tray," Gran explained. "I thought I'd freshen it up for him, but then I had trouble opening a new bag of litter with this silly cast on. I was going to ask you or Harper to help me, but it just slipped my mind. I left it on the counter in the utility room. So the poor little love didn't have anywhere to go."

"Oh…" Mum said.

Harper glared up at her. "You see! It wasn't Sammy's fault! I told you it wasn't! I said he was upset!"

"Harper, just go upstairs, please. I don't have the time or the energy to deal with you being rude. Upstairs! Now!"

Harper ran out of the room and Sammy watched her go, his ears flattened miserably. He could hear her stomping up the stairs – his whiskers shook with every thump. Where was she going? Why was everyone so angry?

Mum bundled the rug up carefully and walked to the door, stopping to open the window on the way. "I don't think it went through to the carpet. If we air the room out, it should be OK in a little while. I'll go and put this in the wash and sort out that litter tray."

"I'll make us some tea," Gran said, following her out, and Sammy was left alone in the living room, shivering and sad.

Chapter Five

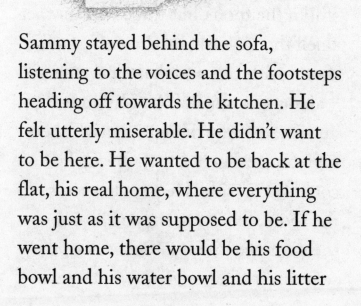

Sammy stayed behind the sofa, listening to the voices and the footsteps heading off towards the kitchen. He felt utterly miserable. He didn't want to be here. He wanted to be back at the flat, his real home, where everything was just as it was supposed to be. If he went home, there would be his food bowl and his water bowl and his litter tray, all in the right places, he was sure. He was so confused and worried that he thought Harper would be at home too – ready to play with him and let him snuggle up next to her on the bed. She wouldn't be grumpy and loud, like she was here.

He had to get back home. Somehow.

The smell of the spoiled rug was still in the room, but there was another smell too. A fresh, bright waft of air, mixed with cars and damp pavements – an outside smell. If he could *smell* outside, Sammy thought, his whiskers twitching excitedly, then maybe he could *get* outside. He prowled across the room, following the smell, and then jumped up on to the back of the sofa to get a better view. Yes, there!

The window was open – wide open!

Sammy hardly thought at all,
he simply jumped, leaping to the
windowsill and
taking a deep
sniff of outside.
He was down
in the flower
bed below the
window in
seconds, loving
the feel of the
crumbly earth
under his paws.
He glanced back up
at the window, wondering if
anyone had noticed he was gone, but
all was quiet. Sammy padded across
the little front garden and slipped

through the bars of the metal gate.
Out on the pavement, he paused,
sniffing thoughtfully. All he knew was
that he wanted to go home – he hadn't
thought about how he was going to get
there. But some instinct deep inside
him was sure of the way to go. He
knew where home was.

Sammy glanced back at the house
one last time, uncertain for a moment,
but then he scurried away down
the pavement. He could hear cars
rumbling by in the distance – and then
one coming closer, along the street.
He pressed himself back against the
garden wall, feeling the buzz of the
passing car under his paws. He had
been out the front of his old home a
few times, but he'd always preferred

the network of gardens and alleys at the back of the flat. It felt quieter. Safer. He wasn't used to cars and now his whiskers were tingling with worry. Perhaps he should go back – it would be easy to jump up to the windowsill and slip inside. Another car rumbled past…

Sammy shook himself impatiently. It didn't matter. He would stay safely away from the cars. He knew his home was waiting for him and he was on his way to find it.

Harper lay on her bed with her face buried deep in her pillow. That way she could growl furiously about how

unfair Mum was, and how unfair
everything was, and
how she wanted
to go home, and
probably no one
could hear her.
She kicked her
feet against
the duvet,
drumming
them up and
down – and then rolled over with a
sigh.

Mum had put that duvet on her
bed the day they moved. She'd chosen
Harper's favourite cover, with the
unicorn kittens. Her fleecy blanket
was there too, folded up by her pillow,
because Mum knew Harper liked to

hold it while she was going to sleep.
Mum had made sure the blanket was
at the top of a box, ready for Harper on
that first night at Gran's house.

Gran… Harper sighed again. Gran
really did need them. She'd seemed so
happy this week, even though her arm
was still painful. She didn't seem as
tired, either. She'd loved having Harper
and Ava to chat to at breakfast, telling
her all about school.

Maybe Harper had been a bit unfair
too?

Mum was so worried about Gran
and she'd had to pack their whole flat
up, and in between doing all that she
was on the phone sorting out changing
their address with everyone, and
organizing the movers, and letting the

school know what was happening

It was a lot. Sammy weeing on the rug wasn't actually the end of the world, but perhaps it had felt like it was?

Harper sat up, hugging her knees and wondering if she should go downstairs and say sorry to Mum. Someone needed to feed Sammy too – he was probably upset about weeing in the house. Harper went to the door, opening it quietly. She could hear Mum and Gran chatting in the kitchen, and they didn't sound cross. She would go and give Mum a hug, and apologize.

Mum and Gran both glanced up as Harper came into the kitchen – Gran was smiling, but Mum looked worried and Harper's stomach twisted inside her.

"I'm sorry, Harper. I shouldn't have

shouted at you," Mum said.

"I came down to say that!" Harper went to put her arms round Mum's shoulders and lean against her. "Are you really upset with Sammy? He didn't mean to…"

"Of course not, it wasn't his fault. I'm just a bit tired." Mum sighed. "We should give him his tea, shouldn't we?"

"I'll do it." Harper got the bag of cat food out and looked around, smiling, expecting to hear a thunder of tiny paws as Sammy came running. But there was nothing. He must still be really upset.

Mum was looking out into the hallway too, frowning a little. "Do you think he's hiding behind the boxes? He probably didn't like us arguing."

"I'll check." Harper put the food in

71

Sammy's bowl and then went out into the hallway, wondering if he was down the side of that basket again. But there was no sad kitten face peering back at her. Perhaps he was still in the living room?

There was no smell, Harper noticed when she went in, so that was good. Then suddenly, something cold seemed to squeeze Harper's insides. The smell had gone because Mum had left the window open. It was still open now, letting in a nice fresh breeze. Harper ran over to it, hoping that somehow it was only just a crack, too narrow for Sammy to wriggle through – but she knew it wasn't.

"Mum!" she yelled in panic. "Mum, the window's open!"

"Yes, I know, I had to let some fresh

air in," her mum called back, and then there was a moment of horrified silence and Mum raced down the hall. "Oh no…" she muttered. "I didn't even think. Sammy! Sammy!" She looked around frantically.

"He isn't in here." Harper gulped. "I think he's gone out of the window, Mum!"

"It'll be OK." Mum patted Harper's arm, but she didn't sound very sure.

"What's happened?" Gran came in and Ava hurried down the stairs to see what was going on.

"Sammy's gone!" Harper turned round from the window. "We left the window open and we were supposed to be keeping him in. We have to go and find him!"

"He's probably just exploring the front garden," Gran said soothingly.

Harper dashed to open the front door and then ran out into the garden. "Sammy! Sammy!" she called. She was trying to keep her voice calm and friendly, but she could hear it squeaking with panic. They'd been going to let him out slowly, with someone there watching him and snacks to tempt him back. Now it had all gone wrong. "Sammy, where are you? Mum, can you see him?"

"Not yet," Mum murmured. "Shhh a minute. Let's listen for him…"

They stood frozen on the grass, hoping to hear the jingle of the tiny bell on Sammy's collar or maybe a confused little mew. But there was no sound at all in the garden – only a car growling by on the road outside the fence.

Chapter Six

Sammy had gone a good distance now, he thought. The kitten could tell he was getting much nearer to the flat and no one had tried to stop him making his way there. He would be back home soon and everything would be right again, he was sure. He would stretch out on the sofa by the window and watch the people and the cars passing, safely far away.

But which way next? Slowly, Sammy twitched his whiskers and then sniffed the air. Yes, he needed to head down here. He trotted briskly along the pavement, wondering if Harper would have a bowl of food ready for him when he got to the flat. He was starting to feel very empty, as if he hadn't eaten for far too long.

The next road shocked him out of thoughts of dinner, though. It was far bigger than any of the small side roads he'd crossed so far – cars were speeding along in a steady stream, with hardly any gaps between them. The wild roaring frightened him and he couldn't tell how fast they were moving – they seemed to be far away one moment and then screeching past him the next. How was he ever going to get across that?

It seemed a very long way to the far pavement, but he was almost certain that home was somewhere on the other side of the road. It felt so close, but he wasn't sure he was brave enough to cross.

Mum and Ava and Harper searched
for Sammy for what felt like hours.
They went up and down the street
calling for him, while Gran stood on
the patio in the back garden shaking
a packet of Sammy's favourite treats.
They stopped to grab a quick sandwich
for tea, but Harper just tore hers
into little bits and nibbled on them.
Her throat felt too dry with worry to
swallow. Sammy was only a kitten – he
was so little! How could he manage
out there on his own, when he didn't
even know where he was?

"He'll probably pop back through the
cat flap any minute, Harper," Gran said.
Harper knew that Gran was trying to
be comforting, but it didn't work. How
could Sammy come back in through

Gran's cat flap when he'd never even been out of it? He didn't know Gran's garden! He didn't know that this was his home to come back to, Harper thought, trying to sniff back tears. She wasn't even sure he wanted to come back. He hadn't liked it here – and he hadn't loved them enough to want to stay. That was the worst thing of all.

Mum and Harper went searching for Sammy again after tea, while Gran helped Ava get ready for bed. It should have been interesting, getting to walk around the streets close to their new home, and have a look at the playground at the far end of the road, but it was horrible. Especially when every time they passed someone they had to say they'd lost their kitten, and he was very little, and please could they tell Mrs Allinson at number forty-four if they saw him?

"We should do posters," Harper said miserably. "With your number on, Mum. Then people could just text you if they saw him."

Mum looked uncertain. "Maybe... I'm hoping that your gran's right, though, and he'll come home by himself. He could be really close, just a bit scared and hiding out. Or he might be shut in someone's garage. Let's give it till tomorrow to start putting posters up. Your gran's already rung all the neighbours to ask them to look out for him." She sighed. "It's getting dark, Harper. I think we need to get back home."

Harper
slipped her hand
into Mum's.
Both their hands
felt cold and Mum
looked as worried
and miserable as she
did. If only they hadn't
argued!

*I'd have noticed the
open window if I hadn't
stomped off upstairs,*
Harper thought
miserably, wishing she could go back
and do everything differently. "Do you
think he *will* come back by himself?"
she asked, and Mum hugged her tight.

"I don't know, sweetie. But I'm
hoping. I'm really hoping."

As the night darkened, the passing cars blinded the kitten with the glare of their lights and they seemed to roar louder than ever. Sammy stayed tucked away under a bush at the edge of the road. The hissing of the tyres left him feeling shaky and scared, and he didn't dare face the road. He huddled down in the dust and dry leaves, flinching each time a car passed, until he fell into an uneasy sleep.

He woke up as the sky began to lighten early the next morning and peered cautiously out at the road. He hadn't felt a car rumble by for a while and everything was very still. The air smelled fresher and he stretched out his paws, wincing at the stiffness after a night on the cold road. Home was very near now. If he could drag up the courage to dart across, he would be almost there.

Sammy edged forwards to the curb of the pavement and then out under a parked car. He couldn't hear anything coming.

Go! Now!

He dashed out, racing faster than he ever had before, and flung himself to the pavement on the other side. He bounded under a thick hedge, breathing hard but delighted with himself. He'd done it! And now... He turned his head slowly. *This way? Yes...* He scampered along the pavement and round a corner, following that strange

instinct inside him. His huge ears were
held high with excitement. He would
be home soon and Harper would be
there, in the right place where she
should be. She'd feed him his breakfast;
he was really, really hungry. Then she'd
let him sleep in her lap, or perhaps
snuggled between her and Ava on the
sofa… There it was! The flat and his
front window.

Sammy galloped happily down the little path that led to the back of the house and nudged at his cat flap in the back door. It sprang open and he dived through, eager to find Harper and his breakfast.

But it wasn't the same.

He knew it as soon as his paws hit the kitchen tiles – there was a strange smell in the air. Some of the furniture was still there, he remembered when he'd scratched that table leg. But there were new things too. That trolley full of vegetables just next to the back door – that hadn't been there before.

It was the smell that was so wrong, though. The flat didn't smell like Harper and Ava and Mum. It didn't smell like *him*. Sammy edged backwards towards the cat flap as he realized. There was another cat here. His flat wasn't his any more, he thought, looking around in horror – and then he saw her.

Perched on top of the fridge and glaring down at him. A massive black cat with bright golden eyes. Every hair of her was fluffed out in fury and Sammy thought she must be at least six times as big as he was. She was hissing now, a long, slow, angry hiss – and then she stretched out her fat black paws down the front of the fridge and leaped. Sammy cowered as she landed in front of him, still hissing, and then he turned and hurled himself at his old cat flap, scrabbling at it in a panic as he heard the black cat yowl behind him.

Sammy shot out into the garden, back arched and all his fur on end. He could see the other cat watching through the cat flap, but she didn't seem to be chasing him. Not yet, anyway. He scurried back down the path to the street and raced along the road, too scared even to think. At last he spotted a big wheelie bin in an alley down the side of a shop and ducked underneath it to catch his breath. What was he going to do now?

Chapter Seven

Harper woke up that morning with an
odd sense that something was wrong.
It took her a moment to remember
what it was, especially as her new room
still felt strange. She reached down
to stroke Sammy – and discovered
that the warm lump next to her wasn't
Sammy, it was Ava.

Then she remembered everything.

Ava was there because Harper had woken up in the middle of the night to find her little sister crying and pulling on the sleeve of her pyjamas. Harper hadn't been able to make out what Ava was saying for a moment – she was too muffled up with tears – but then she'd realized that it was, "I want Sammy back!" She'd let Ava climb into bed with her and held her until she cried herself to sleep.

"Hey…" Mum had pushed the door open and was smiling at her. "I couldn't find Ava and I guessed she'd be here. Sorry, Harper, I didn't hear her wake up."

"It's OK." Harper looked up at Mum hopefully. "Is Sammy back? Did you check his blanket?" Gran had suggested last night that they put Sammy's favourite blanket out on to the doorstep, so he had something familiar to smell if he was trying to make his way back to the house. Harper had gone to sleep thinking about waking the next morning and seeing Sammy curled up there, waiting for them to find him.

Mum sighed. "No. I'm sorry, sweetheart. Not yet. I did look."

Harper wriggled out of bed, trying not to wake Ava. "Shall we make posters?"

Mum nodded. "OK. You start making some. I'll get breakfast ready."

"Emma? Harper?"

That was Gran calling from her room. Harper glanced up at Mum in surprise. Both of them went to look round Gran's door. "Are you OK, Gran? Did you want something?"

Gran was sitting up in bed, with a book in her hand. "I'm fine, don't worry. But I had a thought. Before you put up posters, you should go and check the flat. Maybe Sammy went there? I've heard stories about cats being able to find their way back miles and miles, and it's only ten minutes

94

away, isn't it?"

Harper's eyes widened. "Yes!" she yelped, and then remembered Ava sleeping and put her hand over her mouth, whispering through her fingers. "Oh, yes! Gran, that's got to be right! Can we go now, Mum?"

Mum shook her head. "Not yet. It's too early, especially as it's Saturday. We'll have to give it a while. But that's a great idea, Mum."

Harper nodded, though the thought of waiting was horrible. "I'll make the posters, just in case. But I bet he'll be there and we won't need them after all! When we come back with him I can tear them up into tiny little pieces." She could see herself doing it – or screwing them up into a fat papery ball for Sammy to chase.

Harper had made six posters by the time Mum said they could go, with beautiful cats drawn on them, and a description of Sammy, and Mum's phone number at the bottom. She kept looking between the kitchen clock and the front door, desperate to head back to the flat. At last Mum nodded at her and Harper flew to grab her jacket and her trainers. Ava was still asleep upstairs, but Gran said she'd listen out for her.

Harper wanted to run all the way back to the flat – she kept darting ahead and having to circle back to Mum. Every time she wanted to say, *He will be there, won't he?*

Mum had brought the cat carrier with her, so she must think they were going to find him. But it was hard to imagine Sammy working his way back through the streets, especially crossing the main road. Harper wouldn't want to cross it on her own, so how could Sammy do it? There were parked cars all the way along and it was so hard to see. They had to edge out between two cars, and look, and then hurry across.

Harper slowed down again after

that, now they were really close and they were about to know. Suddenly she was scared.

"Come on," Mum murmured, squeezing her hand. "It's going to be OK, Harper. Even if they haven't seen Sammy, we'll go back and put your posters up. We'll find him."

Harper nodded, but she was holding her breath as Mum rang their old doorbell. It seemed ages before anyone came to the door and then a tall man stood there, smiling at them politely.

"Hi!" Mum said, her voice rather high and worried. "I wondered if you'd seen our kitten? We moved out last week – this was our flat – and he's disappeared. We thought maybe he'd come back..."

"Oh, no, sorry." The man shook his head and Harper felt tears suddenly burn at the backs of her eyes. "What's he like? We'll keep an eye out for him. You want to give me your number?"

Harper stood pressed tight against Mum's side, watching a beautiful black cat stalk out of the kitchen towards them. She was huge and her fur was all fluffed up. Perhaps she didn't like strangers, Harper thought. Or she didn't like the flat, like Sammy didn't like Gran's house.

Harper looked back as they walked away and saw that the black cat was on the back of the sofa, watching them from the window, just like Sammy used to.

It made her want to howl and she had to hold her hand over her mouth. The black cat was in Sammy's place and her little spotted kitten was out there somewhere all on his own.

Sammy peered out at the pavement and the feet passing by. What was

he going to do now? He had been
desperate to find home and now
home wasn't there. He'd expected that
everything would be the same, the
way it should be. Now he knew that
it wasn't. The flat belonged to another
cat instead. He shivered at the thought
of her angry hiss. Did that mean he
didn't have a home any more?

Sammy huddled himself smaller
and tighter. Was he really all on his
own? Or perhaps – had he been
looking for the wrong thing?

It was Harper and Mum who
put the food in his bowl. Ava who
climbed up on the sofa to look out
of the window with him. Harper
who curled herself round him in the
middle of the night and made him

feel safe and loved.

He had to find them. His home was where they were; it wasn't a place at all.

But how? He hadn't got to know the new house. Did he even know how to get back?

Sammy wriggled slowly out from under the bin and set off along the pavement, trying to remember the way he'd come. He'd followed this wall just before he came to the flat, he was sure. But then – his ears flattened. At the end of the wall was that big road again and a car speeding by, the tyres screeching loudly on the tarmac.

Sammy stepped slowly out between two parked cars and stood there, listening. Was it safe to run? The road seemed quiet. He scurried out and then froze in panic for a moment as he saw a car bearing down on him. Sammy flung himself forwards, darting to safety just in time. The car sped on – had they even noticed what had almost happened?

He scrambled up on to a wall, shivering at the memory of the car's hot breath ruffling his fur. He licked a paw and swiped it round his ears and whiskers, over and over again, trying to wash away the panic, until at last he felt a little calmer. Then he jumped down and set off again, slowly retracing his steps as well as he could.

It was as he turned a corner that he noticed a faint, familiar scent in the air. Something that smelled of home… Harper. He hurried on eagerly, hoping to see her any moment, but the street stretched on ahead of him, empty and strange.

Had he gone wrong? But … there was still that scent.

He was so busy trying to catch it

again that he didn't notice the dog
until they were practically nose to
nose – and the dog seemed just as
surprised as he was. It jumped
back, eyes wide and
ears pricked, and
whined. Then it
crouched down,
stretching out its
front paws,
and barked
sharply
at him.
Sammy
retreated,
terrified.
He'd never
been so close to a
dog and he didn't know what to do.

The elderly woman holding the lead pulled the dog back. "What's that, Petey? No, leave it alone!"

Sammy hissed faintly and turned tail, racing away through a clump of bushes nearby. He wasn't going to give that huge dog the chance to get any closer.

At last he looked out on to an open stretch of grass, dotted with people. Away over on the other side of the grass, swings were moving through the air and children were calling. Sammy was sure he'd never seen it before. He retreated back under the bushes, feeling so tired. He had no idea where to go next.

"But where is he?" Ava demanded, staring at Mum and Harper over her bowl of cereal. She'd woken up while Harper and Mum were back at the flat and Gran had told her where they'd gone. Now she just couldn't seem to understand why they didn't have Sammy in the carrier.

"We don't know at the moment," Mum tried to explain. "We'll keep on looking, though. Harper's made posters. We'll go and put them on all the lamp posts soon. If anyone sees Sammy they'll know to call us."

Ava only shook her head. "We have to find him. He'll be hungry. He's missed tea *and* breakfast."

Harper pushed her cereal round her bowl, blinking back tears. Ava was right, of course. She was too little to know that it didn't help to say it. "I've finished my cereal," she told Ava. "Let's go and put the posters up now."

"Give me half an hour, Harper, OK?" Mum said. "I've got the numbers for all the local vets and the animal shelter. We should call them first, to see if anyone's found Sammy and taken him in."

Harper nodded. That made sense. "I'll make some more posters then. Or can I go and start putting them up?"

"And me!" Ava jumped up from the table.

"No, not on your own. I'll be as quick as I can, I promise. I know it's hard to wait, but it's important to call the vets. Someone might have found Sammy already."

"I'm going to make posters too," Ava said, grabbing a piece of paper and starting to draw a kitten, but Harper followed Mum into the living room.

"Mum, can't I just go down the street and put some of the posters up? It's not far and I won't cross the road."

Mum sighed, looking at her phone and the list of numbers she'd written. "OK. But only as far as the end of the street, all right? Don't go past the park."

"I promise." Harper nodded. She knew Mum was right, and someone might have found Sammy already, but she just couldn't bear waiting any longer. She kept thinking of her kitten out there, lost and confused, and it made her stomach twist up inside her.

Chapter Eight

Harper stopped at the entrance to the park, wondering if she should stick a poster up on the fence. Lots of people would see it there, but she wasn't sure how well the tape would work. She held the poster up against the wooden slats, frowning. Perhaps there was a noticeboard or something like that at one of the other gates.

"Are you all right, dear?"

Harper turned to see that an elderly couple with a dog had paused on their way out of the park. She nodded shyly. "I was going to put up a poster," she explained. "Our cat's missing. He's a kitten really, a grey tabby kitten."

"Oh!" The woman glanced out towards the road. "A silvery colour? With spots?"

"Yes!" Harper nearly dropped the posters. "Yes, he's spotty! Have you seen him?"

The couple nodded at each other. "We did see a little cat. Petey scared him, I'm afraid," the man told Harper. "He's friendly, but the cat didn't know that of course. We were back up the road that way and then the cat ran off, into one of the gardens, I think." He pointed up the road towards Gran's house.

"That was about fifteen, twenty minutes ago?" the woman put in. "I'm sorry we didn't see exactly where he went."

"But you saw him!" Harper smiled shakily. "Thank you! I'll keep looking."

"Good luck finding him!" the man

called back, waving to her as they set off up the street.

Harper leaned against the fence for a moment. Sammy was OK! They'd seen him – a spotty silver kitten – it had to be him, didn't it? She hurried back along the road, calling hopefully. "Sammy! Sammy, here, boy! Where are you?" She was sure that she'd see him darting out of a garden towards her any moment, but she went on calling and calling, and nothing happened.

He could have gone further up the street, Harper decided, especially if it had been a while. She ran along the pavement, stopping to peer over fences and under cars, always calling.

About halfway between the park and their house she saw something grey

dart underneath a gate and she gasped
excitedly, running to lean over and look
into the garden. "Sammy! I'm here,
Sammy, come on!"

There was a moment of silence and
then a little face looked back at her
from behind a tall fern.

It wasn't Sammy. The cat looked a
bit like him, but it had a white chin
and paws, and it was mostly striped,
with a few spots along its sides. It just
wasn't her kitten. Harper swallowed
hard, gulping back her disappointment.
She'd have to keep looking.

She was turning away from the
garden when she realized the awful
thing. The elderly couple must have
got it wrong. They must have seen *this*
cat. Young and thin and silvery tabby –

it all matched.

No one had seen Sammy after all.

Under the bushes at the edge of the
park, Sammy startled awake.
He'd heard a voice
he recognized.
That was
Harper, he
was almost
sure. She was
here! She was
calling him! He
leaped up, racing
to the edge of the path,
and then checked, looking around for
the dog. He remembered its bright

eyes and the way it had snuffled after him so eagerly. Sammy's tail fluffed up to double size again. What if it was still there, waiting for him? He was safe here underneath the bushes – out there he'd be in the open, with nowhere to hide. He crouched under the low branches, hesitating.

But he had to follow Harper's voice. He couldn't let home go again!

Sammy darted out on to the path and through the park gates to the street, hoping to see Harper looking for him. But no one was there.

Harper rubbed her eyes on her sleeve. She knew crying wasn't going to do any good, but she couldn't help it – she'd been so excited, so sure that she was about to get Sammy back. That extra little bit of hope from the elderly couple had been torn away, leaving her feeling more heartbroken than ever.

She would go back and see how Mum was doing with the phone calls, she thought sadly. Maybe there'd been some good news. Then she looked down at the poster in her hand and sighed. It had actually been a sensible idea to put one up at the park – so many people went through those gates. She just needed to find a better spot than the fence, that's all. She'd do that now, rather than wasting the poster.

"I can't give up," Harper muttered to herself. "We're going to find him.

We have to." But she wasn't calling for him as she trudged back down the road towards the park. She wasn't hoping, the way she had been before. She walked on with her head down, just concentrating on not crying.

She was unrolling the poster, ready to tape it to the litter bin by the gates, when she heard the mewing – high, frantic, excited mewing. She dropped the poster and the sticky tape, without even noticing that she'd done it. She looked around wildly, her breath caught in her throat – and a tiny silvery spotted cat came racing out from under the bushes by the park gates.

"Sammy!" Harper scooped him up into her arms. "They *did* see you! I thought – oh, it doesn't matter!

Where did you go? We have to get back and tell Mum. She's calling everyone about you. Oh, I dropped the poster!" She scrabbled around to pick it up, while Sammy tried to climb inside her jacket and nuzzle her, purring and purring. Then she shoved the poster into the bin and whispered into the top of his furry head, "Let's go home."

The house still seemed a little bit strange – but Sammy was starting to feel as if he belonged. His litter tray was in a nice quiet corner now and his toys were scattered everywhere. A blanket that smelled like Harper was draped over the back of the sofa. He could stretch out on it and see the street, and watch the birds in the garden too.

When Harper had carried Sammy into the house, such a wave of happiness and relief had swept over him. He could feel them all loving him – Harper, Ava, Mum and Gran. He'd followed them around all day, even curling up in Gran's lap under the table while they were eating lunch.

That night, as Ava and Harper had started up the stairs, Sammy had put one paw on the bottom step and mewed. "He wants to go with you!" Mum had said to Harper, laughing.

"You'd better help the poor kitten out," Gran agreed, and Harper had scooped him into her arms again and carried him up to bed with her. He'd investigated the bathroom while the girls were brushing their teeth and then followed them back into Harper's room. He liked this room – there was a windowsill and he thought it might be sunny to sit on tomorrow. So many different places to explore up here. So many interesting smells.

Now he yawned and stood up, turning round a couple of times and padding at the duvet to get it just right.

"Is he OK?" Ava sat up in bed to look at him worriedly and Sammy nudged his nose against her cheek.

"I think so." Harper smiled at her. "He does that, Ava, it's all right. He's getting comfy. Go to sleep. Mum said you could only come in with me if you promised not to keep chatting."

Ava lay back down, and Sammy tucked himself into the nest of duvet between both sisters and started to purr. Some things were different, but this hadn't changed. This was where he was meant to be, curled up with Harper and Ava.

Harper rubbed her hand gently over his ears and he heard her sigh sleepily. "Don't worry, Ava. Sammy's back home."

Out Now

From MULTI-MILLION best-selling author

Holly Webb

The PUPPY Who Ran Away

Illustrated by Sophy Williams

Out Now

From MULTI-MILLION best-selling author

Holly Webb

Nadia and the Forever Kitten

Illustrated by Sophy Williams

HOLLY WEBB

Holly Webb started out as a children's
book editor and wrote her first series for
the publisher she worked for. She has been
writing ever since, with over one hundred
books to her name. Holly lives in Berkshire,
with her husband and three children.
Holly's pet cats are always nosying around
when she is trying to type on her laptop.

For more information
about Holly Webb visit:

www.holly-webb.com